This book belongs to

_____

This book was donated by
James Alty
Dover, NH

Published by AMITY Publications
www.amitypublications.com

Charlie and The School Bully
Copyright © 2012 by Layne Case
ISBN: 978-1-934582-53-4
Library of Congress PCN 2012920045

AMITY Publications
37 Rogers Run
Barrington, NH 03825

To contact Layne Case or to order a copy of this book, please visit
www.amitypublications.com

Design and layout by
Nancy W. Grossman
170 Mechanic Street
Portsmouth, NH 03801

Printed in the United States of America

Charlie
and
The School Bully

Written by Layne Case
Illustrated by Pat Sciacca

Charlie came to live with the Whitneys when he was just six weeks old. He was a cute little puppy, with big floppy ears and huge paws.

As Charlie grew older, his tail grew longer. In fact, it grew to be three feet long!

Charlie tried to be careful, but his tail kept getting him into trouble. One time, he broke Mrs. Whitney's beautiful lamp from Paris.

Another time, Charlie's tail tripped Mr. Whitney. Boy, was he angry at Charlie.

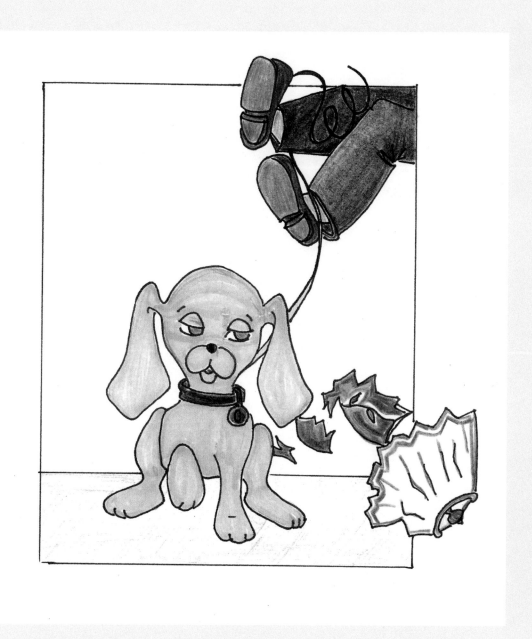

So, Mr. Whitney finally decided it was time for Charlie to attend Puppy Kindergarten. He thought it would help Charlie learn to be less clumsy and follow commands.

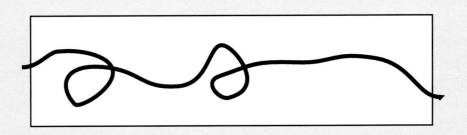

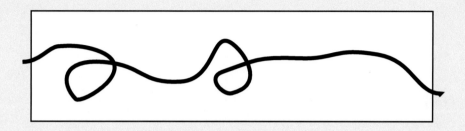

Charlie was not very happy about
this. He wasn't a puppy anymore, but
he was also a little scared. He had
heard how tough school would be.
Plus, he knew there would be other
dogs around.

Charlie preferred to be by himself or with his friends in the neighborhood, like Louie, the lizard who lived next door, and, Meezer, a Siamese kitten who lived across the street.

Charlie didn't have any dog friends. So, the idea of puppy school was pretty scary.

The first day of school finally arrived.
Charlie and Mr. Whitney entered the room.
There were lots of different dogs. None
of them looked like Charlie.

There was a beautiful Collie.
There was a handsome German shepherd.
There was a large Great Dane.
There was a little Chihuahua.

But, there wasn't one dog in the room with a tail as long as Charlie's. All the other dogs noticed how different he looked. Some made nasty remarks about his "stupid tail."

Charlie wanted to go home. This was not going to be fun.

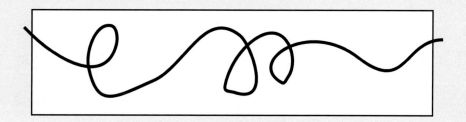

Mr. Whitney found a space next to one of the smaller dogs.

As the teacher explained what they would be learning, Charlie noticed a large dog nearby.

This large dog was a mean looking dog. He had a long snout, a thick body, and was all black, which made him look very scary. He was staring at Charlie, bearing his teeth, and growling.

Charlie heard the owner yell, "*Bruno! No!*" Charlie knew he was going to stay away from him.

The next week, Charlie and Mr. Whitney arrived a little early. They stood next to that same small dog. Charlie introduced himself.

"Hi. I'm Charlie. What's your name?" he asked.

"My name is Durango," said the small dog.

"Durrrrrangoooooo! I like that name! Makes me think of the old west," said Charlie. "Durango, the toughest dog this side of the border!"

Durango laughed. "Yeah, well, don't be fooled by my name. I'm not very tough."

Charlie noticed that same mean dog across the room. He was growling at all the dogs who came near him. His owner kept yelling, "*No, Bruno!*" Charlie was hoping Bruno wouldn't notice him.

The following week, Charlie saw Durango and made sure to get a spot next to him. However, Bruno was right next to Durango. Durango was cowering behind his owner's leg.

Bruno leaned over Durango and growled at Charlie.

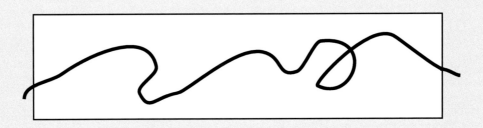

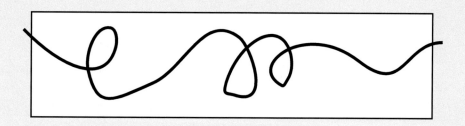

Every week, Charlie would look for Durango. And, every week Bruno would be right next to him, making sure Charlie couldn't get too close, always standing over Durango, growling.

Durango was so frightened, he barely looked up when Charlie said hello.

One week, Bruno wasn't there. Charlie saw Durango standing next to the door, watching every dog as they entered the room.

"Hey, Durango. How are you?" asked Charlie.

"I'm okay but I hate coming here," replied Durango.

"Really?" asked Charlie. He could guess why but thought it better to ask. "Why do you hate coming here?"

"Every week, Bruno makes sure he stands next to me," said Durango. "Then he spends the entire time telling me how stupid I am, that I'm never going to pass the class. I tried staying away from him, but his owner and mine have become friendly, so they always stand next to each other."

Durango looked around. "Looks like he's not here today," he added, with a sigh of relief.

"No wonder you don't look forward to school," said Charlie.

"Oh, but there's more," Durango added. "Sometimes Bruno bites my tail, which makes me yelp. Then my owner yells at me, thinking I'm the one who's misbehaving."

Charlie felt bad for Durango. He didn't know what he could to do help him. If Bruno was biting Durango tail, Charlie certainly didn't want Bruno to bite *his* tail.

The last week of class, Durango didn't show up. Bruno was there, only now he stood next to a little poodle. Bruno had found a new victim.

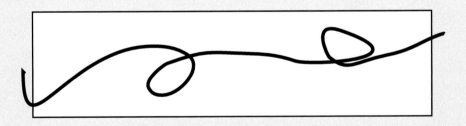

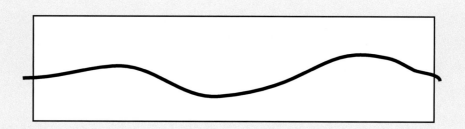

Charlie thought a lot about Durango, wondering what may have happened to him. He wished he had said or done something to stop Bruno, but he was just too afraid himself.

Charlie thought about Bruno, too. What would make him pick on Durango? Why was he so mean? Had someone treated him badly?

A few weeks later, Charlie was walking around the neighborhood. He headed down the road to the cul-de-sac. There in the middle of the road was a large "bump."

As he got closer, he could hear a low growl. He wasn't sure what to do. He hadn't learned how to defend himself in school, just how to sit, stay and not pull on his leash.

He walked slowly toward what he finally
realized was another dog, crumpled in a heap.
"Grrrrrr," said the dog. Then, "Yelp."

"Are you okay?" Charlie yelled from a distance.

"*Grrrr*," was all the dog would say.

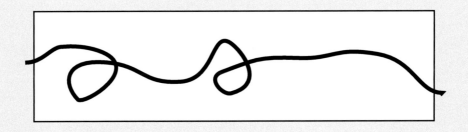

As Charlie got closer, he suddenly recognized that growl.

"Bruno? Is that you?" asked Charlie rather timidly.

Bruno lifted his head slightly. "Oh, no...not *you*," said Bruno.

"What happened?" Charlie asked.

Bruno whimpered a bit, clearly in pain. "I was chasing this boy on a bike and he ran into me, knocking me over. That stupid kid! I think my leg is broken," he said.

Charlie stepped a bit closer. Sure enough, Bruno's leg was broken. Charlie didn't want to leave Bruno in the middle of the road. It was getting dark and he worried Bruno wouldn't be seen if a car came down the road.

Charlie thought for a moment, then wrapped his tail around Bruno's collar. Slowly, he pulled the big dog over to the side of the road. Bruno was trying not to cry, but the pain was almost too much to bear. Once Charlie got Bruno to the side of the road, he asked Bruno where he lived.

Bruno pointed his nose toward a gray and white house that sat back off the road. Charlie ran up to the front door and barked until someone opened it.

"GET OUT OF HERE, YOU DIRTY MUTT! GO HOME!" the man who opened the door yelled.

Wow! Charlie wasn't expecting that. The man didn't even know Charlie. But Charlie barked and barked, running back and forth from the house to Bruno. Finally, the man saw Bruno and ran out to him.

The man started yelling at Bruno, calling him stupid. He sputtered about how much this was going to cost to have his leg fixed. He picked up Bruno, not very gently, which caused Bruno to cry out.

Then he plopped the big dog in the back of his truck and drove away.

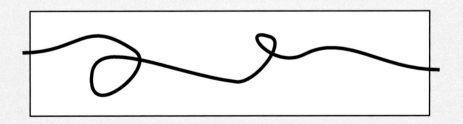

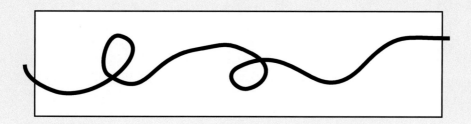

Charlie thought...poor Bruno. He now understood why Bruno was so mean. He'd learned it from his owner.

A few days later, Charlie headed down the cul-de-sac to see if he could find Bruno. There he was, lying on the front porch, his leg in a cast.

Charlie went up to the porch steps and quietly called his name. "Bruno?"

Bruno opened his eyes and glared at Charlie.

"How are you feeling?" Charlie asked.

"Okay. My leg still hurts but I should be up and about in no time, chasing bikes again," said Bruno, a bit sarcastically.

"Bruno. Maybe it's time to stop chasing bikes and start chasing butterflies. They can't hurt you. And..." Charlie stopped. "And...well, it's just not nice to be mean to others, Bruno. Do you remember Durango?"

Bruno nodded.

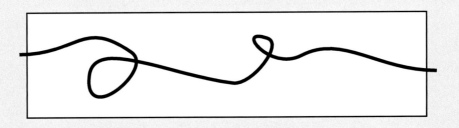

"He never did finish school because you scared him so much. You called him names and kept biting his tail. That really hurt him. I mean...how do you feel when someone calls you names?"

Charlie stopped, then said quietly, "I heard your owner call you stupid. Bruno, you're not stupid. In fact, I think you're pretty smart."

Charlie smiled, trying desperately to think of something to say to prove it.

Bruno closed his eyes. He had started to cry. No one had ever spoken so kindly to him. And, he could tell Charlie was really concerned about him.

"Thanks, Charlie," Bruno said. "I really appreciated your help the other night. And, I appreciate you stopping by today. You're right. I shouldn't be so mean. Look where it got me."

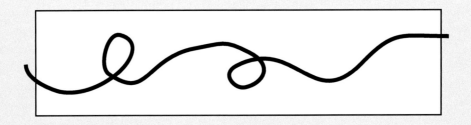

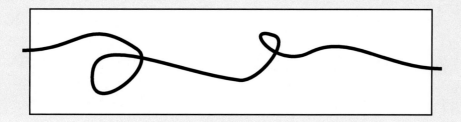

Charlie smiled. He knew Bruno had a good heart inside. He just needed someone to show him how to use it.

Once Bruno's leg healed, Charlie and Bruno started walking around the neighborhood together. Charlie introduced Bruno to some of his other friends.

Louie, the lizard, was a bit scared of Bruno. He was so much bigger than Louie.

Meezer, the Siamese kitten, thought Bruno was a pony and jumped up on his back.

Charlie and all his friends gather together when they can. Charlie and Bruno keep an eye on the neighborhood. Bruno is now known as the neighborhood "Police Dog." And, Charlie is his "partner," long tail and all.

The End

68067462R00031

Made in the USA
Middletown, DE
14 September 2019